Queen Midas in Reverse

DIANE RINELLA

ISBN: 0692593861
ISBN-13: 978-0692593868

For N. Stevenson Jennette III.

Acknowledgements

Every now and then a writer gets lucky enough to have someone enjoy her work and ask for more. At the repeated badgering, I mean request, of my friend, N. Stevenson Jennette III, I could not say no. He is the reason you are about to read Jacqueline's story.

To my Modster Squad, a dedicated group of fans who make me feel like I'm a thousand times better than I am.

By personal law I need to acknowledge The World's Greatest Stalker, Darla Roybal. She motivates me when my inner spirit fails.

My kindred spirit Steve Stone. When it comes to music, he is Niles to my inner Rosalyn. Our conversations inspire much of the banter in the *Scary Modsters* universe.

Last, and in no way least, my husband, Brian Preston, and our daughter, Trishalana Rinella Preston. Thank you for tolerating my ups, my downs, and my all arounds.

Love Stinks

Jacqueline

Friday nights always seem to be an angel that wears a devil's tail. Even though we swear we are going to try someplace new, my friends and I always wind up at Mulligan's. Coming here has turned into a ritual—like dragging your butt out of bed at five in the morning to go to a job where you feel underutilized.

Seriously, of all the bars in Los Angeles, I don't get why we hang out here. Maybe it has something to do with feeling like you are at a place where everyone knows you. I feel like I live here, and I don't come here half as much as Rosalyn and Darla, as this also serves as the after-hours spot for their co-workers from Endeara Candies.

Somehow though, this once cozy, neighborhood bar that has been transformed into a synthetic version of a Victorian era lounge is comforting. This makes zero sense because it often draws the type of clientele that drives us a little batty. I think we are still in love with the Mulligan's of old—the one that reeked of used-up, nineteen-fifties charm. When the area was redeveloped, it was transformed into a beautiful, albeit a little tacky, pick-up club.

If I'm totally honest though, my friends and I aren't just fixtures here because we enjoy each other's company. All of us, at one time or another, have wanted to find Mr. Right. That seems unlikely in a place like this. I mean, why hang out somewhere frequented by guys who are obviously not your type? The thing is, it has worked for my friends, so it is not unrealistic to think that it could work for me.

A few months back Darla met her boyfriend, Chris, here. He walked in, took one look at her blue, green, and purple hair, and nearly sprinted over to the table. Within five minutes they were laughing at all the crazy things they had in common. I felt witness to two souls being reunited.

Then there's Rosalyn—my quirky best friend whom we call Rox. The nickname was given to her by her dad as a homonym for her favorite genre of music. Back when we were knee high to tadpoles, our dads were in a band together. Wherever Rosalyn's dad went, she followed. In turn, my dad always brought me to keep her company. Rosalyn and I have been through everything together; the loss of both of her parents, losing my grandma, my parents nearly divorcing, and most recently, the disappearing act her ex-boyfriend did when their infant son died. You name it and we've supported each other through it.

To look at us you'd think we were opposites. That's because while I am somewhat of a slave to modern fashion, she often wears Day-Glo. Yep! My best friend has a fetish for times before she was born. Usually she is dressed like she just walked off of Mary Quant's runway, circa nineteen sixty-six. You know what? She looks the part, perfectly. You know what else? I'm totally jealous. As much as she struggles with her sense of self, once she puts on one of those old dresses she comes alive. Me? When I try on that stuff I look like a kid who should be given a Trick-Or-Treat bag.

A few weeks ago, Rosalyn met her boyfriend, Niles, here. Niles seems to be her perfect match. He randomly showed up one night with a business associate. Rosalyn dared to put herself on the line and ended up meeting Mr. Right. I can't help but think that someday it's going to be my turn.

The first round of drinks arrives at our table. Immediately we raise our glasses. "What are we drinking to tonight?" Darla asks.

"To the fact that Jacqueline looks smoking hot!" Rosalyn adds.

"What are you talking about, Rox?" Darla asks. "Even with barely any makeup on, with those blue eyes and silky, onyx hair, Jacqueline always smolders. It's a miracle you and I ever get any attention."

"Isn't that the truth!"

Lord, with how colorful those two are! "Are you kidding? Between Darla's peacock mane and Rox's Day-Glo dress it's hard to miss you two."

Darla and Rosalyn whip their heads toward each other and snicker. They then look back to me, again in unison, but Darla is the one who speaks. "Did you ever think that we have to do this because next to you we look like the most unattractive people in the world?"

I change the subject before the girls can seal the toast with a sip. As much as I appreciate the compliments, I'd rather move on to something else. "To the fact that my two best friends are crazy."

Rosalyn senses how self-conscious I am and slips me a smile. She then shifts the attention to Darla. "So what was the big commotion between you and Oliver at work today? I heard he flipped your files around."

Darla smacks her hand on the table. "Oh no, it was far worse than that. He took the first file in my top drawer, removed the contents, then swapped them with the contents of the last folder in the bottom drawer. He then proceeded to do that with each file so only the one in the middle had the proper stuff in it. Three drawers! Three whole drawers of refiling! Unbelievable!"

I take another sip of my drink while shaking my head at the craziness of Darla's work situation. This is what happens when people are not allowed to work to their full potentials.

Laughter from a group of guys across the room grabs my attention. They seem rather happy-go-lucky. That is, all but one of them. He's mostly looking at his beer, but occasionally he glances up and lets out a reserved chuckle. He doesn't seem troubled but more out of place—like he has other things he'd rather think about. He also has a really nice smile.

"That's okay," Darla says. "I already have a plan to get back at Oliver."

"Of course you do," Rosalyn adds. "I can't wait to hear

this one."

One of the guys from the rambunctious group tells a joke. I can't make out the details, but it comes off as being condescending to women. The nice guy looks up, gives a polite smile, and sips his beer. He didn't seem to appreciate the joke much. This makes me appreciate him.

"Well," Darla continues. "It's not very devious, but it will be kind of fun. You know how he's always using pens to color code stuff, like what client he talked to about which product and the day of the week he's promised deliveries? I'm going to swap the insides around. When he picks up the red pen it will actually be purple. The blue one will be green."

Rosalyn laughs. Her long, brown locks shimmer as she bounces in her seat. "That will drive him absolutely crazy, especially if he doesn't realize it until he is on the phone and has to make a note. I can't wait to hear his rant over this one!"

The guy with the nice air about him heads to the bar for a refill. There is nothing about his appearance that makes him my type. I like guys who are tall and handsome in a bit of a pretty yet rugged way. This man is short, got a couple of extra pounds around the middle, and his hair is thinning. However, I find his demeanor fascinating. I want to meet him.

But I have a second date with Jeff tomorrow. Should I really do this?

Seriously, Jacqueline, no wonder why you are still single at thirty-one. You have a *second* date tomorrow with a guy who had such a hard time making eye contact that seeing him again goes against your instincts. Under those conditions, a simple hello to someone else hardly implies you're a bad person.

I down the rest of my drink and turn to the girls. "I'm ready for another. Anyone else?"

These girls know me all too well. All eyes go to the bar and see nothing that they think would interest me. When they turn back, both of them cock their heads as if asking why. It's a little weird. We can't help it though. When alcohol starts creeping its way into our systems we tend to act in sync.

Rosalyn's eyes glance back to the bar. A slip of a smile

forms on her face. "Looks like we're good for now."

I take a moment to straighten my skirt before heading off. I'm always concerned I'll accidentally be one of those girls whose skirt rides up and shows what color her underwear is, which is one of the many reasons why most of my dresses come to around my knees. I also take a moment to make sure my blouse is buttoned above the cleavage line because sometimes the top button pops open. I seem to do the exact opposite of what other girls do. I guess this is yet another reason why I am still single.

I head to the bar and stand next to the guy who sits while waiting for his beer. Harold, the bartender, hands it to him while addressing me. "Hey, Jacqueline. What can I get you?"

"Hey, Harold. Another of the same, please. Thanks."

I slip the guy next to me a smile. He looks straight into my eyes and smiles back. That doesn't happen very often. Usually a smile is followed by—

His eyes scan downward, pausing briefly on each of the three points of my curves. Damn.

Well, it's not like we girls don't check out guys, too.

I say hello. He returns the greeting before his eyes go to his beer. Now I am even more curious. I check to make sure he is not wearing a ring before continuing. "I've never seen you here before. Are you new to the neighborhood, or are you just visiting?"

His eyes meet mine again, and he keeps a polite smile. "I'm here with some friends."

"Me too. This is kind of our Friday night, hangout place." His gaze is distant, maybe a little detached. He isn't making this easy. Okay, one more piece of small talk. If he doesn't warm up, I'll leave him alone. "I work in the marketing department for a news network. What do you do?" I leave off the part about it being for Sporting News Today. I really don't know more about sports than I need to. However, guys assume I am going to try to one up them, and sometimes that is a turn off. That and how I constantly need to do things five times better than any of my male counterparts is ridiculous.

"Marketing? That's clever." His eyes scan my body again. "I should really get back to my friends." His brushoff comes out hesitantly, leaving me feeling even more awkward.

"Enjoy your night," I tell him before returning my attention to Harold as he makes my drink.

The guy turns back to me. "Look, you're a gorgeous girl and all, but I'm here to have a good time with my friends. If you're here every Friday, then maybe next week we can do some business. Just not tonight. Sorry. I'm sure I'll regret it later."

Business? He thinks I'm a prostitute?

My gaze goes to my outfit. The most skin that shows are my arms from the bicep down. The length of my skirt reveals only the top of my knees to my calves. My cleavage is still almost fully covered. This outfit doesn't make me look cheap or tarty. Either my sense of self-image is totally wrong, or this guy is just a prick. "I believe you have the wrong impression." My voice sounds indignant.

"Look, lady, you can stop with the sale. I'm not buying."

My jaw drops. I know it's stereotypical, but it's what happens. I try to keep from causing a scene, but restraint is a little hard. "What the hell? How dare you?"

In a flash, Rosalyn is by my side. "Jacqueline, what's wrong?"

The guy takes a good look at Rosalyn who is wearing a paisley dress and go-go boots. He looks at me again and shakes his head. "This is a really weird fetish thing you all have going on."

"I'm fine, Rox. This man seems to think that I'm trying to sell him something—that something being me. I was just trying to make small talk with someone who looked like a nice guy. Apparently I was wrong."

As if I don't want to sink into the ground enough, now Harold dashes over. "Jacqueline, are you okay?"

No, I'm far from okay. This isn't the first time something like this has happened. Even though I hardly looked like a whore last time either, Rosalyn had to stop me from tossing out half of the contents of my closet. This time I know I don't look like a tramp. How can this guy think that?

Now that Harold has stood up for me, my words seem to have merit. The guy's expression changes from unimpressed to embarrassed to the point of actually going a little red around the edges. He sets down his beer and motions for me to take a seat. There's no way I'm doing it.

His eyes look to the ground. "I am very sorry. I'm not used to women making small talk with me, especially ones that are as pretty as you. Naturally I came to the conclusion that you were looking for something else. Call it bad self-esteem on my part. It doesn't excuse my behavior, and for that I am truly sorry."

"Come on, Jacqueline." Rosalyn tugs at my arm for us to go back to our table but no. I need to know what's going on. Why isn't this the first time? What is it about me that gave this man that horrible impression? My eyes start welling with tears, but I am determined to stay calm because getting information is far more important than letting out my aggressions. "Why did you think I was a prostitute? Was it something I said? Is it the way I'm dressed? If I'm doing something that conveys that, I want to change it. Please be honest."

The man shifts, looking awkward. Finally his eyes race up and stare straight into mine. This is the honest man that I saw sitting with his friends. "It wasn't a single thing you did," he says. "The truth is, you're the type of gorgeous woman that walks into a room and every man takes notice. You are also the type of woman that every man feels he could never have. You came from out of nowhere and started talking to me. Let's face it, I'm no prize. As much as you weren't exactly coming on to me, I had to question why a woman as pretty as yourself would bother looking in my direction, even if just for small talk. Really, it's not you, it's me, and I mean that sincerely. I am also truly sorry."

What can I say to that? I can't say it's okay because it's not, but he's truly upset with himself. Lack of self-esteem makes people do a lot of stupid things. I get that. "Thank you.

Apology accepted." I head back to my table without giving the guy another look. I am going to sit with my friends and pretend this little event never happened. Well, at least I'm going to pretend it for now, because I'm sure it will haunt me later.

When Rox and I get back to the table, Darla is off keeping the guy's friends at bay. She comes back fuming. "I can't believe those guys! Are you okay?"

Lord, what now? "I'm fine. What are they saying?"

"Nothing that a brainless idiot wouldn't blurt." Darla grabs her purse. "We're out of here."

I take my seat. "Nope. I'm not going to let a little stupidity ruin my night. I look how I look, and I look like me."

Harold comes to check on us. "You ladies okay?"

"Yeah, we're fine," I tell him.

"Stay put, okay? Another round of drinks is coming for you, courtesy of the idiot. The one after that is on me. If you pass on that extra round tonight, the credit carries over to next Friday."

I start to refuse the drinks, but why should I? Because I feel bad about how that guy hates himself for his ridiculous mistake? Because he has self-esteem issues that make him think he is not worthy of having a conversation with a pretty girl? Let him pay.

"You're a trooper," Rosalyn tells me. "I know you won't let this break your stride." I force a smile. Her tone implies that she is proud of me, but I know Rosalyn, and her eyes convey her concern.

"But?" I ask. She looks at me blankly before those big brown eyes soften and shy away, so I finish for her. "But sometimes we all wonder just how far we should be expected to go to secure Mr. Right. Well, at least you two seem to be set. Everyone has their hurdles, right?"

We stay and enjoy our drinks while doing the best we can to laugh away the effect of the bad incident by looking at other guys and joking about our jobs. Yet when all is said and done, I walk out of the bar while wishing I could scrub off my face and look like someone else.

❊

The second Rosalyn and I are through the door of our home, I slip off my shoes. When I rise from grabbing them, I find her staring at me.

"You good?" she asks.

"Yeah, I'm fine. Go call Niles. I know you're absolutely dying to." She gives me a sideways glance. My every move is under scrutiny. "I'm *fine*. Go call your man."

"My man!" she squeals before dashing off. Geez. I swear those two nut cases could not be more perfect for each other. Shoot, if somebody as goofy as Rosalyn can find a match like Niles, there's hope for anyone.

Why is finding a decent guy so hard? The problem has to lie with something that I do. I know I am attractive. That may seem egotistical, but every woman should admit what she truly knows about herself, both the good and the bad. For better or for worse, I'm pretty. I could try to hide that by wearing muumuus, frizzing my hair, and wearing makeup that makes me look sick, but none of that would be me. I am whom I am—an attractive girl who likes to dress well. There is nothing wrong with that, so the problem must be with my personality.

Then again, tonight I barely got out a hello before being shot down.

I grab the remote and curl up in bed with the hope of finding a great movie. Movies either suck me in or help me discover uncharted territory in the recesses of my mind by providing a visual background and a score for my own story. However, when I really need to escape and fear where my wandering mind may take me, I turn to a book. Books help me live another person's dream.

I happen across the original *The Manchurian Candidate*. It's perfect. *The Manchurian Candidate* always transports my brain into a world of controversy.

Frank Sinatra appears on my screen, looking young and handsome. Even though the film is in black-and-white, my mind sees his blue eyes.

That guy tonight, he had blue eyes—really pretty ones.

They also looked sad when he realized his mistake. I kind of feel bad for him.

Wait a second. Why do I feel for a guy who insulted me? I'm also forgetting, a little too rapidly, that that guy mentioned possibly meeting me next week to pay me to have sex with him. Yeah, Jacqueline, you really know how to pick them!

The TV gets switched off. The remote is exchanged for my Kindle, and I turn my mind off to the rest of the world.

Not Fade Away

Rosalyn

"Oh, man. These look amazing!" Niles says of the bacon burgers placed before us. I'm with him. All those caramelized onions with the pepper jack cheese are to die for.

"I'll be right back with your hot fudge," the waitress says. She gives Niles the same look of disbelief she did when he placed his order. "You did say you wanted hot fudge, right?"

"Yes, please." The waitress starts to head off and he calls back to her, "Excuse me, can I please have a side of warm peanut butter, too?"

The waitress smiles awkwardly before looking at me. I'm pretty sure she is sending me a telepathic message that the cute ones are always a little nuts. I just smile.

I don't know that I'll ever get used to the way Niles eats. It's not that there is anything wrong with it. It's just that it's, well ... odd. I mean, I know I am an odd character and am in no way one to talk, but seriously, I just don't get it. Chocolate on fries is strange enough, but now he is adding peanut butter into the mix?

Actually, the peanut butter should overpower the oil from the fries and make it more like eating peanut butter and chocolate on a soft cracker. Maybe it will even be cookie-like. Okay, I am totally game.

Niles puts his elbow on the table and rests his hand in his palm. He then stares at his fries and releases a sigh of longing. A tuft of his brown hair slides over his green eyes that seem to constantly be aglow with discovery and wonder. It's so adorable. How someone in his early thirties can look so manly yet also so boyish seems contradictory.

I try to divert his attention to something more engaging than his grumbling stomach. "Beatles or Stones?" I ask.

Niles's eyes shoot straight to mine, and he straightens his back in attention. "Seriously? You want to risk going down that road?"

"Sure. How bad can it get? It's kind of a no-brainer." Not only that, but us talking about this should be like most people when they chat about the weather. With his level of hunger and need of a diversion, I should have come up with something more challenging.

"Yeah, no-brainer is right. Stones all the way."

"What?" almost screams out of me. "Are you crazy?"

The waitress arrives with bowls of hot fudge and warm peanut butter. She may have just answered the question for me.

Niles goes for a fry and dips it into the hot chocolate. He chews it with a smile toward heaven that makes me think he has reached bliss. I try not to gag. Maybe I don't want to try that with peanut butter after all.

Oh, why not? I grab a fry and go for gold. Niles's eyes widen when he sees me dip it in the chocolate and then the peanut butter. "Oh God, that's brilliant. I need to try that."

The peanut butter sticks to the roof of my mouth while the chocolate and the fry mush together. No, this is *not* brilliant. Not at all!

Niles follows my lead. "Hey, not bad!" He then flags down the waitress and asks for more peanut butter. I want to tell him that I really don't need more, but I'm too busy reaching for my soda to wash it down.

I don't know what is worse, the bad food combo or the fact that he thinks the Stones are superior to the Fab Four. I finally get my mouth cleared enough to talk. "Okay, you have some serious explaining to do." He looks to the peanut butter. "No, about your side of what I did not expect to be a debate. How could you possibly pick The Stones over The Beatles?"

Niles dips a fry into the chocolate. "Well, for starters, they have a better logo." He then pops the fry into his mouth like the case is closed.

The sound of my phone vibrating comes through my purse. Whoever it is can wait. In my mind, this conversation is more important than a meeting of The United Nations. "That makes zero sense. The Beatles didn't have a logo, unless you count the one for Apple Corp."

"You just proved the point. The Stones had a logo, so that is one in their favor. Two, they used the same logo for their record label. Seeing that tongue spin around is far better than watching an apple. And since we are on the subject of what the Stones have that the Beatles did not, Jagger and Richards have a cool nickname. Lennon and McCartney are just plain old Lennon and McCartney."

He's certifiable! "Just plain old Lennon and McCartney? Those names are synonymous with brilliance. Besides, who even knows The Glimmer Twins anymore?"

The waitress leaves him another bowl of peanut butter, thus driving home how crazy he is. Seriously, he must be nuts.

Niles grabs a spoon, takes the top off of his burger, and scoops the peanut butter on it. It is times like these that I wonder if Niles does things for shock value. Thing is, I know this is just him. I kind of love it. In fact, I'm finding I love a lot of things about him.

I may need to take a risk and steal a bite of that burger.

Okay, but seriously, "The Beatles did everything first. They fawned over American music and covered Chuck Berry first. Also, the brilliance of *Sgt. Pepper's* came before the wannabe-in-the-same-league *Satanic Majesties*. The Beatles were innovators while The Stones are practitioners." Again my phone buzzes. I probably should check it, but I just want to enjoy my date. I reach across the table and go for a bit of Niles's burger. My teeth sink in, and I brace myself for the impending terror.

The warmth has caused the peanut butter to break down and melt. It blends with the bacon and caramelized onions and … Holy St. Lennon, this is fantastic!

"My point exactly," Niles says. "The Beatles did it first, but

The Stones are doing it last. You can't argue with that."

I go for the other bowl of peanut butter to create my own delicacy. Okay, he may have been right about the burger, but he is wrong about his side of the debate. "That means The Beatles knew when to call it quits. Did we really need *Black and Blue, Voodoo Lounge,* and *Bridges to Babylon*?"

Niles doesn't even bat an eye. "You may have a point, but after The Beatles bailed The Stones gave us *Sticky Fingers* and *Exile On Main Street*, which you have to admit are genius." Again my phone buzzes. Niles looks to my purse. "Maybe you should get that."

"Are you conceding?" He's right. It is odd for my phone to go off so many times.

"Over this? Never. I'm a lawyer. We don't concede unless we have something to gain."

As soon as I see who the missed calls are from, my heart sinks. "Oh no."

"Something wrong?"

"Three missed calls from Jacqueline. She's supposed to be out on a date." Niles does not even hesitate before insisting I call her.

Jacqueline answers just after the first ring. Her disappointment transmits over the phone before she even gets her first word out. "How much would you hate me if I asked you to come get me? I called for a cab, but they are backed up and will take about two hours."

"Two hours! Where are you?"

"Griffith Park."

"What! What are you doing all the way out there?" Heaven love him, Niles is already signaling the waitress. He hands her his credit card and asks for our food to go. I mouth, "I'm sorry." He waves his hand and tells me it's fine.

"It's a long, long story," Jacqueline says. The poor thing sounds crushed. "Can you come get me? I'm really sor—"

"Say no more. We are on our way."

Niles's Camaro pulls up and stops right in front of the bus stop I told Rosalyn I was near. She jumps out and starts screaming for me. I swear the fear in her shrieks could wake the dead. Now I really don't want to face anyone. I should have continued to handle this alone, but being out here by myself doesn't feel safe.

I emerge from behind a bush, and Rosalyn runs toward me like I am returning home from war. I sort of am. Her welcome hug is like a death grip. I keep telling myself I am tough and can handle anything. While that is somewhat true physically, I'm not sure how much more my heart and self-esteem can take.

Niles holds the back passenger door open for me while scanning the area for trouble. "I'm sorry for ruining your night," I tell him.

He gives me the shyest smile. "My night? I now get to escort two beautiful women. I'd say I'm the envy of the state."

How great of a catch Niles is gets driven home when he doesn't close my door and open the front one for Rosalyn. They have only been dating a few weeks and he already knows her well enough to suspect that—

Rosalyn slides into the back to sit next to me. "What in Hades happened? Are you sure you are okay?"

I shrug. "I'm okay." Her eyes scan my body, looking for signs of a struggle. Now I am really glad that I did not fall when I ran. I have got to stop wearing heels on dates. "Really, I'm fine."

Niles gets into the driver seat and whips us out of there. After we get down the road and pass the gas station from where I just fled, I release a breath that I wasn't even aware I was holding. Finally, I turn to Rosalyn, who has been patiently waiting for me to fill her in but not pushing in case I don't feel comfortable talking around Niles. It's sweet, but right now I don't care who hears.

I blurt out, "I don't get men."

She tosses up her hands. "Who does?" In the rearview mirror I catch a glimpse of Niles as he eyes the back seat and then tries to go back to minding his own business. Still, he can't hide his look that says he doesn't understand the members of his sex much either, nor does he understand us. Why can't all guys be like him?

Rosalyn puts her hand on my arm and leans her head into my shoulder. Funny how sometimes when I need someone to lean on, and don't know where to start, she gives me strength and direction by leaning on me.

My first date with Jeff was sweet and G-rated. I didn't get so much as a peck on the cheek goodnight. Now I see that was just a front so I would trust him.

I've had it with guys and their games. It shows in how I burst forth without a filter. "Remember how I told you that the entire time we were on our first date Jeff was nervous, played with his napkin, and didn't want to look me in the eye? Dinner tonight was a total replay. Once we were on our way to a club and had no food to distract us, I tried to get some conversation going by talking about happy childhood memories. Seems simple, right?"

Rosalyn nods. "Yeah, harmless." Then she grips my arm. "Oh, no. You didn't tell him about when we were sixteen and your mom berated our dates for not bringing us corsages for the junior prom, did you?"

"How would that lead to him ruining our date?"

"It ruined theirs!"

I shake my head. "No, not nearly right. I told him about how my klutzy father tried to teach me how to ride a skateboard and nearly broke his tailbone. Mom was already bent over how he was going to get me killed just by going down to the next driveway."

"That's a happy memory?" Niles asks.

"No, but it became one when he gave up and my uncle

took over. He had me racing down hills in no time. We almost took out a group of third graders." The memory makes me laugh even now. "Lord, you should have seen them scamper! Anyway, I asked Jeff about a happy moment he had. That's when all went to hell in a Port-A-Potty. You know what he said? He asked me if I liked three-layer cake?" Rosalyn looks as perplexed as I did by the question. Meanwhile, Niles shifts in his seat. I point to him. "See? You men! I swear." Niles starts to open his mouth and then slams it shut. Poor guy. He seems to know that when women get going, men don't have a chance. "Sorry, Niles."

He smiles. "It's fine. I'm just glad you are okay."

God, that's sweet.

"I don't get it," Rosalyn says. "He gets happy over cake?"

I watch Niles try to swallow back a snicker.

"That's what I thought," I say, "so I asked him what kind of cake he liked. I went so far as to say that I have a thing for carrot cake as long as it doesn't have nuts. Suddenly Mr. Sweet and Nervous looked me dead in the eye and said 'Pussy.' "

Rosalyn's eyes go wide. Poor Niles keeps his straight on the road. You could not read his expression if it were typed on his face.

"Jeff then went on to explain that when you have three girls all stacked up it's like eating a three-layer delight. His big goal in life is to get to four layers, but you need the right kind of girls because a really thin one needs to be on top. The one on the bottom needs padding so she will be less likely to get crushed!"

Niles turns on the radio at a low volume so as not to be rude. Softly he hums along to distract himself from the conversation. Smart man.

"You have got to be kidding!" Rosalyn shrieks.

"Oh, hold on. I'm not at the best part yet. So he went on about how he had a couple of girls that could join us and asked if my roommate would be home tonight." Niles's head snaps toward the back seat. He's clearly none too happy at anyone even thinking about disrespecting Rosalyn. "That's when it got weird," I continue. "He said that even if I could not persuade you, we had to go to my place, because his, um, *roommate* would be home and she could not know what was going on. Normally, he wouldn't say anything, but he wanted to be honest with me so I would not get too attached. He told me he still lives with his ex-girlfriend and even though she says they are done, he knows they will eventually get back together."

"What?" Rosalyn asks. Her brows are raised so high that I expect them to pop off.

"Exactly! I should have bailed then. Instead, I let curiosity get me and asked why he was out with me if they were on a *break*. He said that after the first two years he got tired of watching her with other men and figured he should have some fun of his own."

Rosalyn's jaw drops. "They've been broken up for two years *and* he still lives with her *and* thinks of it as a break?"

"Wait, it gets better. So he wanted to skip the club and go straight to my place. I figured I would play along and have him detour by Darla's to *get her* at which time I would forget to come back outside. We stopped for gas, and I was in the process of calling her when Jeff's cell phone chimed with a text. When the screen lit there was a picture of a woman and a cute little boy of about three. You know what the text said? 'On your way home from poker, please pick up more medicine. Jimmy's fever just got higher.' Funnily enough, the sender was female and had the same last name as he does. Granted, that text could have been from his mom, but then another one came through from the same person that said, 'At least the cold medicine should knock him out so we can finally have some alone time.'"

"No!" Rosalyn says. "Is that when you took off?"

"No, he was on his way back to the car, so I sent him back inside for some whipped cream so his snack cake could have filling. Then I took a picture of the cell phone with the wife's name and number showing. After I bailed and called you, she was my next call. When he gets home, he has one hell of a surprise coming!"

Niles pulls up to the house. Before I can unbuckle my seatbelt, he already has my door open. Once we get to the porch he asks, "Should I head home, or would you like me to hang out on the sofa for a bit, just in case you get a visitor? He did pick you up from here, right?"

"I don't want to ruin your night. Why don't you two—"

"No way!" Rosalyn objects. "I'm not leaving you alone."

"I'll be fine," I assure her. "Besides, there is no way that guy is coming here. I scared him off for good."

Niles shows that his concern is as great as ever. "I'm not so sure that a call to the wife of a guy like that constitutes scaring him off for good."

"Niles is right," Rosalyn says. "I'm not feeling too good about this." She motions us all inside. If I don't level with her about the rest, she'll probably start calling everyone in my family to come over and build a fortress.

"Look, Rox, I didn't want to freak you out, but he saw me leave the car and chased after me. I warned him to stay away, but he didn't listen, so I showed him I meant business by doing the only thing I could. I maced him." Just the thought of it makes Niles scrunch his eyes and rub them. "Oh, I didn't get him in the face. Mace goes through clothing. Imagine how it felt when it hit his balls."

Niles squirms and jerks his leg over his man parts, finally putting a smile on my face. "Yes!" Rosalyn exclaims. She high fives me then slips me some skin and adds in a hip bump.

I head off to make us cocoa, and although I am smiling, my heart still sags. I'm trying to have the best attitude possible and to not let my faith in finding my happily ever after slip, but it gets harder with each disappointment.

Rosalyn heads upstairs to change and Niles joins me in the kitchen. "You really okay?" he asks.

"Yeah, I think I need to quit the dating game though."

In the short time he and Rosalyn have been together I've have not gotten to know Niles much. However, he feels like an old friend when he sucks in his lips and takes a moment to ponder before speaking. "Trust me on something. The worst thing anyone can ever do is give up on themselves. We all have our challenges, and while sometimes they are greater than what meets the eye, the only one you have that I see is bad luck. Bad luck is not a reason to give up. When you give up, not only do you lose, but the rest of the world never gets a chance to see who you are. Would you ever let Rosalyn give up on who she is?"

Something about Niles's sincerity puts me aback. For the first time I wonder who he really is inside and what has shaped him to be the seemingly perfect misfit match for my best friend. "No, I never have, and I wouldn't dream of it."

"Then don't give up on yourself."

Rosalyn comes back downstairs and drags Niles into the family room to help her pick out some music. Something behind those green eyes of his just raised my curiosity. We all have challenges. I would think that his are based on his quirky personality, but something now tells me that the sweet Niles has troubles of his own. I used to just be happy that Rosalyn found someone, now I find myself wondering what he has gone through and am happy for him that he has found her.

Relationships are a two-way street. Out there is a man who is having a tough time of it, just like I am, and wondering when I will come along. I won't give up on finding him, and I won't give up on being myself.

Born Under A Bad Sign

Jacqueline

When the going gets tough, the tough get signed up with a dating service.

That does not seem like anything a tough person would do.

Clearly I have lost my marbles. I always think that Rosalyn is the nutty one, but if someone as quirky as she is can score a match like Niles, there has to be hope for me, right?

This must make me a masochist, or at least certifiable, but Niles was right; I will never find what I am looking for if I give up.

With my laptop in hand I head into Rosalyn's room. She needs to tell me I'm not crazy. Shoot, I'd settle for hearing I am nuts if it helps me get some semblance of peace.

Rosalyn is lying on her bed, listening to The Hollies while reading an issue of *Shindig!* with them on the cover. If the vintage rock posters that line her walls do not sell the scene enough, the fact that she is in wild eyeliner and a dress that makes her look like she should be a dancer on some sixties TV show does. I love my eclectic best friend. She always strives to be herself, no matter what others may think.

I lie down next to her. As soon as she finishes her paragraph, her eyes turn to me. "Be honest," I say. "I just joined a dating service. Have I totally lost it?"

A smile that is so sympathetic that it is almost maternal crosses her face. She tucks her head into my shoulder, and now I feel like I am the strong one. "There is nothing wrong with wanting more out of life, just like there is nothing wrong with wanting someone to share it with."

"True, but I am beginning to feel like a serial dater. When should I say enough is enough?"

Rosalyn props herself up on her elbow. "Jacqueline, you are my rock when I flail, which is more often than I'd like to admit. You are also one of the strongest, coolest-headed people I know. You just have the misfortune of being a magnet for jerks."

"Gee, thanks. With a rave review like that I should have given up years ago."

Her board-straight locks sway as she shakes her head. "No, listen to the first part of the statement. You are a strong person—meaning you are going to get through this. If anyone can weather this storm, it's you."

I really want to think she is right. "But signing up for a dating service? I always thought that was for people who are desperate." My heart sinks at how personal that statement feels at this moment. Why is it so wrong not to want to wake alone every morning? "I hate admitting it, but I guess I have joined that club."

"Think of it more as not willing to settle for less than you deserve and having the courage to seek it. Dating services exist because people like you are having a hard time. That's all."

Still, I can't help but wonder if I am doing the right thing. Then again, nothing else has worked, so why not try this?

Rosalyn motions me to give her the laptop. "Okay, how about I help you? Let's be picky but open-minded. Knowing you, he should be somewhat career oriented, yet also a free thinker and not all about work. He also can't be intimidated by a strong woman who may know more about sports than he does."

Gosh, why do people always think I know so much more than I do? I never mention sports, do I? Great, now I am scrutinizing even more of myself. "I'm just a marketing person for the network, not a news caster. It's really not that big of a deal."

"Yes, but men don't always see it that way. Besides, time and again you have had to prove yourself at work in order to get ahead. That freaks some men out."

I can't help but sigh. Yeah, knowing more than men in some areas might be part of the problem. But what about all the bad dates where we don't even mention our jobs? What about the guys who are just after one thing? Why would being a strong person make guys think I would be an easy lay? Wouldn't they expect the opposite? Maybe they see me as a challenge.

"Ooh!" Rosalyn nearly squeals. "Check this cutie out! Look at all that gorgeous hair and those tight pants!"

I sneak a peek at the guy whose photo must have been taken in the eighties. "We are looking for someone for me, remember?"

Her gaze slips away just long enough to give me a grin laced with guilt and giggles. "Sorry, but he is cute." Rosalyn resumes her search. "Wait! Here!" She shows me a guy who looks like heaven dropped him from a cloud. "He is totally your type," she says of the man with the dark hair, green eyes, and grin of a used car salesman, minus the sleaze. "His name is Bobby," she continues. "He lives in Pasadena, is a writer for a women's magazine, and has an art gallery as a side business. How cool is that? He can't have hang ups about stereotypes if he writes for a woman's magazine. Why not give him a shot?"

She clicks the message icon and starts typing. I nearly jump out of my skin with panic. It's not that I don't trust my best friend; I'm just not so sure I should do this. "Oh, no you don't! I'll send my own message."

"You won't know what to say." Rosalyn keeps typing. I swipe the laptop from her. Her message reads, *Hi, would you like to meet for coffee?*

"Don't you think that message is a little bland?"

"Yep! It's short and to the point. It also means you don't have to spend the next forty minutes freaking out over what to say and then wondering if you somehow put your foot in your mouth. All of your info is already on there, so just click send and be done."

She's right. My profile reflects who I am. Attaching a dissertation on my merits is pointless. Besides, why spend time on a sales pitch when I haven't even spoken to the guy to see if we click? I suck in a breath and click send.

Rosalyn bounces while clapping. "Yay! This is exciting."

She's crazy. My best friend is totally crazy.

Then again, why not be optimistic?

"Come on, let's keep looking!" she says, nearly ripping the laptop out of my hands.

"Rox, don't you think one at a time is enough? I may be open to meeting people, but I'm not really up for—"

She lets out a squeal. Like she darn near squeaks. "Look! Did you see this red dot up here? You've got a message. I wonder if it is from that Bobby guy already!" She races over to click on the icon. "No!" she says while flapping her hand at my arm. "It's another guy! Oh! Look at him! He is handsome!" I start to lean in and look, but she jerks the laptop away. "Wait, you are totally color blind when it comes to people, right?"

I shrug. "I've never thought about it, so yeah, I must be, that is, as long as he's not green. Well, Mediterranean, olive green would be great, but I draw the line at aliens. Although at this point … Seriously though, it makes no difference to me."

She hands me the laptop. "Great! Look at him. He is so handsome. Raymond Jones, thirty-three, six foot two, and check out those cheek bones! Why don't you take a peek at his profile?"

Rosalyn is right; the guy is really handsome but "Um …"

"What?"

"Well, it says he has a degree in Humanities but has a job with the postal service. Doesn't that seem a little odd?"

"It sounds like code for an actor or poet who needs a day job. He may not be a good fit then, because you are drawn to professional, suit types."

I stare at the profile. A weird sensation crawls over me. The reason for it has to be how I am second-guessing this dating service thing. I also have nothing in common with this guy.

I need to get past my hang up about doing this, because while I may not see a reason to say yes to his request to chat, I see no reason to say no. What harm could come from a coffee or lunch date?

Though Rosalyn smiles at me, her face is scrunched up. She knows I'm hurting and how badly I want to be happy. "Do you think I should take a chance?" I ask.

"Only you can decide that, but I will say that every time you put yourself out there, be it for a guy who seems like he would be perfect or for the most unlikely candidate in the world, you are taking a chance. Do what you feel is right for you."

That's exactly what I would say to her. I'd also be hoping she would go for it.

Oh, why not? The second I start typing, Rosalyn starts peering. I reply to the guy with my number and tell him I would enjoy talking to him. I hit send and again she squeals. I join her. Life is about adventures and risks, so I should embrace them.

She jumps off the bed, turns up her stereo, and nudges me to dance. I'm in. Dancing like a fool with her sounds way better than concerning myself over what lies ahead.

Girl All The Bad Boys Want

Jacqueline

Whenever I go out, be it on a date, with friends, to work, or to the library, I always make sure my phone is fully charged and that I have enough cash to get home—just in case my only option is a cab with a credit card reader that is out of order. My mother instilled this habit in me long ago. In light of my last date, I have added to the list that unless I am with Rosalyn, Darla, or a family member, I will always take my own car. I am not a paranoid head case, just a woman who is annoyed that life has taught her to be this way.

Raymond sounded so sweet over the phone that I agreed to a dinner date. He doesn't seem to be anywhere near my type, but lately the type of guys who interest me have been the biggest losers on the planet. Broadening my horizons can't possibly be bad.

I slip out of my car and smooth my pants. Unlike my normal date attire of something dark and sleek yet covering, I opted for navy blue pants, a baby pink, satin blouse, and a string of pearls. When Rosalyn pulled the ensemble out of my closet I thought she had lost the last marble she had left, but then I caved to trying it on. I felt cheery and different about myself. It seemed to be the change I needed to boost my attitude, so I stuck with it.

The click of my heels on the cobblestone path sounds different from usual—springier, livelier. My smile builds at the sight of children across the street as they giggle and splash in water that bursts from a broken fire hydrant. The reflections of street lamps coming off of the water on the sidewalk remind me of the movie *Singing In The Rain* and have me feeling like I am dancing to a swinging beat of old. I wonder if Raymond can Swing dance? I've tried and failed, but I would be up for it again. A one-shot dance lesson sounds like a fun second date.

The often lively shopping district is aglow and open for business, yet the bulk of the noise comes from tires treading through water. Raymond leans against a lamppost. He's tall and thin yet somewhat built. He is in an all-black outfit—slacks, button down shirt, shoes, tie, and jacket. The only speck of color is a bright yellow, lapel pin of a happy face. The outfit is both striking and amusing. It also makes him look like he is a well-dressed stagehand. Maybe he has a side job at a theatre. I have to say that I really like the attire, especially that happy face.

"Raymond?" I ask.

He turns, and I get a smile that gleams as much as the signs on the shops. "Hello," he says warmly. I extend my hand to shake his and he slips something into it. The light is so dim that if the rose were not surrounded by white baby's breath, I would not be so sure that I know what it is. "A stunning rose for a lovely lady. I hope it is not inappropriate, but my mother taught me to never greet a lady empty handed. Shall we?" he asks, gesturing toward the café.

We step inside, and the brighter light shows me that Raymond is damned handsome, far more so than in his photo. Score!

The hostess tells us to sit anywhere we would like. Since I promised myself I would take precautions, I grab a table near the front with a nice view of the street along with that of the front door.

The waitress wastes no time in handing us our menus, but I have a hard time focusing on mine. Raymond's eyes rise and catch mine peering at him. I divert mine. He smiles.

Damn, I'm caught. I hope I wasn't ogling. I try to cover. "I have to tell you, I love what you are wearing. I was a little taken aback by the happy face at first, but I honestly find it charming."

Did that sound sarcastic? I really hope it didn't because that little touch is pretty nice.

He smiles and then asks, "What happy face?"

Odd. Maybe he was visiting a kid earlier and forgot he had it on. "The one on your lapel." He looks lost, so I point to it.

"Oh, that … That's not a happy face. That's Nantuka."

"Nantuka?"

"Yes, my guardian spirit."

Not another one.

He smiles in a way that is almost a little laugh. Relief floods me in realization of his joke, yet somehow I feel he is serious. "Well, the pin is not my guardian, but it represents him. Why are you not wearing an image of yours? Don't tell me you forgot on this of all days."

Um … Well, Rosalyn did speculate that he may be an actor and there are a zillion of them in Los Angeles. "On all of what days?"

"Dark Reaping." His tone is as ominous as the name.

"What is Dark Reaping?"

His eyebrows scrunch in the center. Is his surprise over my question or the fact that I am playing along? "Are you serious?" He then eyes the room and pinches his lips between his finger and thumb. He is doing a great job at pretending he is concerned for me.

See what I am doing here? I'm optimistic, because normally I'd be thinking this man has lost it. But no, I am giving him and his sanity the benefit of the doubt.

He shakes his head, and a smile crosses his face. Oh, thank goodness.

He clasps his hands together and looks to heaven. "Oh, what a relief! I am so glad to have met a soul who has not been touched by evil! You! You are exactly what I need to ward off the badness. Most people flip out when they hear about it and thus doom not only themselves but also me further. You, however, are my savior. Still, we have got to get you a talisman, just in case."

He reaches into his pants' pocket and slides something across the table toward me. It makes a scratching noise like it's metal. When he pulls his hand away, I struggle to repress my laughter at the pin of a cartoon Basset Hound. "Here, Carminak will help you."

Raymond is deadpanned, and I struggle to stay the same way. If this is a survival contest, I am not going down easily. "What is Dark Reaping?"

"It is the day that Hothma reaps souls. On this day, once every decade of my thirty-two years on this planet, Hothma has claimed someone close to me. Each year I hold my breath, not knowing if it is the year he will again strike. But now I am starting to think I may be safe. Clearly Lantha has sent me an angel."

Hothma? Lantha? I took a class about ancient gods in college, but these names sound totally made up. Is he serious? Should I Google the names and see if they jive with anything? Even if he is not insane, this is a little much, especially for a first date.

Okay, I need to lighten up. See, maybe the problem really is me. Playing along for a minute can't hurt. After all, we are in public, and I have a charged phone, cab fare, and a fully gassed car a block away. "How come I have never heard of Dark Reaping? Since the day holds so much importance, you'd think it would be on my calendar."

His head rises, and his eyes pierce into mine. "Maybe you are no angel after all. An angel would not dare to disrespect Dark Reaping."

Okay, with that look, now I know he is pulling my leg, and I can't suppress my laughter. Raymond's hands fly to the edge of the table and he pushes himself back. "You dare to laugh?"

"At a made up holiday like that? Yes! Game over!"

He does a great job at looking offended—so much so that I'm starting to buy into it again. "I know three people, three dead people, who would disagree with your sense of humor."

I cross my arms. Yeah, I'm coming off as smug, but this is one zany icebreaker. "And just who were these three people?"

His expression of mortification drops, and his features turn soft and downtrodden. "How can't you believe me?" He swallows deeply, and something about it tears at me. "My grandma died when I was seven. Not a day goes by that I don't miss her. Then my aunt—her daughter and the twin sister to my momma—died on the same date when I was fifteen." A tear forms in the corner of his eye. There is most definitely pain coming from the depth of his soul. Whatever he is using to recall the emotions he needs to sell the game, it's pretty heavy. "Then, when I was twenty-six, my mom died on that same date. You just don't get over something like that."

He dabs at the tear. Now I really hope that every word he has said is fabricated.

"According to your profile," he says, "you work in marketing. You are not involved in nanotechnology, are you?"

"No, television."

He shakes his head. "I don't know if that is any better. You know, all of the women in my family that died, they were involved in some form of communications. Grandma, she invented nanotechnology, even though no one gives her credit. And Mama and Auntie worked in the communications department at NASA. I tell you, there is some kind of alien, electronic waves in the air that caused them to die. You know how they all went? Aneurisms. All three of them."

Okay, NASA, the inventor of nanotechnology, and aliens? This is too nuts for him to be a crazy person, so what is the harm in playing along? "I am very sorry for your losses. If Dark Reaping is today, is it safe for you to be out?"

He flaps a hand and balks at me. "Oh, sure. That is why I am wearing black."

Yep, it's a joke. No one can switch from sorrow to scary like that and mean it. "Black keeps you safe?"

"Yes, it appeases the dark sorcerer who cursed them." He sets his hand on the table, just shy of my arm. "I'm concerned that you are not wearing any black."

"I'm sure I will be fine."

He leans in closer. "Yes, I am sure you will be since we are not close. But if you were wearing some, it might help protect the rest of my friends and family."

"I'm sorry."

His voice softens and turns seductive. "Can you maybe change clothes?"

Say what? Okay, that's it. Sane or not, he's just crossed the line to no longer amusing. "Sorry, I don't have any with me."

"Are you at least wearing black underwear?"

"No."

"A black bra?"

"Sorry." I look toward the door. Stupid me let him sit next to it.

He closes his eyes and moans. "We might want to stop off and get you some. You should be sure to keep them on later."

"Later?" I'm betting this guy could out-run me. I'm glad I sprang for a fresh container of mace.

"Well, with this being Dark Reaping, it might be your last night to experience earthly pleasures. We need to take advantage of the moment." His hand clasps on to mine, but my attention is more drawn to his other one that is sliding up his leg and into the most private of places.

I start to jerk away and catch sight of the rose he gave me earlier. I thought it was red, but no, it's spray painted black. This guy may truly be crazy. If I run, will he chase after me? Should I cause a scene? What happens if I do and he is carrying a gun or a knife?

Maybe I could tell him I have a black jacket in my car and go to get it.

No, he may want to walk with me. Then he will have me alone in the parking lot.

Better yet, I'll slip on a poker face and play his game.

I lean toward him, slide my hand over his, and whisper, "There is a boutique across the street. Last I was in there they had quite the ladies section. How about I slip over and come right back?"

His eyes pop open and scan down to my boobs. Is he drooling? He then looks to the store across the way. "Okay."

He sounds like he's already started playing without me.

I slip my hand through the handle of my purse, trying to act like I am loving every second of dreaming of the wonderful night to come. I then whisper in his ear, "Be right back." I can feel his eyes on mine while I dash across the street and slip into the shop. I make towards the back where there must be a service door.

Suddenly I stop. What if he suspects I am fleeing and has already headed for the parking lot?

I take a moment to browse while weighing my options. I should call for help.

No, that may take too long and he will come looking for me.

The sound of air breaks steals my attention. Just in front of the shop, Lantha has sent me an angel in the form of a bus. I make like the wind and bolt on to it. Tomorrow I'll come back to get my car while armed with a police escort. Knowing I am safely out of here will be worth the parking ticket. Maybe the cops will let me off. I should have grabbed the rose and pin as evidence.

My heart races as I sit down as quickly as possible with my back to the restaurant. Even as we pull away, I keep my head low for fear Raymond will catch on and chase the bus down. However, I'm able to sneak a peek out of the corner of my eye, just as he raises his lapel and kisses the image of Nantuka. I thank Carminak for my escaping Hothma.

I've got to start keeping a diary.

Oliver's Army

Rosalyn

"My God, who is that?" Inside the lobby at work I walk up to Darla as she stares out the window at a beautiful specimen. His deeply toned skin is so smooth it is jealousy inducing. "Damn, his cheekbones are as high as a skyscraper."

"Davion Pense," she says through a breathy sigh. "He applied for a job in the warehouse. You should get a good look at his lips. They are so kissable that I almost jumped across my desk and grabbed dessert. He's also single."

"How do you know that?"

"We had a nice chat while he waited for his interview. He lost his wife of nearly a decade last year and just moved here to start over. He's one of those striving-for-change, never-give-up types that we all try to be."

The smell of cigarettes coming from behind tells me the clicking of the heels I just heard belong to Oliver. It always cracks me up when I think about how much he looks like Cousin Oliver from *The Brady Bunch*. "What are you two looking at?" All eyes remain locked on the target.

"Heaven," Darla says while sounding as if the man is a creature of her dreams.

I share in her revelry. "With the way he's built, it's no wonder he applied to work in the warehouse. He would be perfect."

"Perfect for what?" Even though Oliver nudges my shoulder, it's Darla that gives his arm a playful smack. Here they go again.

"That's a nice thought, but he doesn't have the right forklift license. There's no time to train him, so they went with another guy."

"Bummer." I can't help but check out his ass as he walks to his car. "It would be nice to have a little more eye candy around this place."

Darla rolls her eyes. "You mean *some* eye candy!"

"Hey, what am I?" Oliver protests.

Darla's eyes twinkle with mischief. "A thorn in my side who smokes too close to my lobby while yammering on his cell phone."

"I'd return the banter, but as a male member of the species I have learned not to fight. Instead, I'll just put tape over the earpiece on your phone so you'll think you are growing old and losing your hearing."

"Well, I suppose it's not any worse than the time I used high-tac to stick your stapler to the ceiling." Darla tosses a copy of the dreamboat's résumé onto her desk. "I'm keeping this, just in case we ever need it."

I grab it for a once over. "Wow, he's got a lot of job stability and great letters of recommendation."

"Why can't all guys come with résumés and references?"

"Amen to that, sister!"

Oliver flails his arms. "Hey, hello! Guy standing right here, totally willing to be ogled instead of slammed for being male."

"Tell ya what, Oliver. You help Rox by grabbing this box that one of the managers left on my credenza because he was too lazy to walk to the elevator, and I promise to watch as you do it."

"What? Are you serious?" I turn to find an overflowing Banker's Box of ratty folders. The ridiculousness just never ends around this place. "These are personnel folders." Geez, the candy we make here must be so toxic that even the fumes mess with people's brains.

"Yeah, he was gonna leave them for you in the break room, but then he decided he shouldn't be so lazy and left them here."

How non-chivalrous, not to mention the fact that those should always be under lock and key. How is it that I, a payroll specialist, knows more about employee confidentiality than the managers? I've got to get out of this place.

Oliver takes the box from me as I start to head back to my office. "Here, allow me. If I can't get ogled, at least I can be useful."

As he passes Darla's reception desk he stops and whispers to her, "Hey, thanks for covering for me the other day when I spaced on that meeting. You really saved my ass. Seriously, one slip and I could have lost my job. That would have lost me my kids as well."

Darla waves it off. However, the forty minutes she spent faking to the boss that Oliver was with a client while he was really off trying to patch things with his ex got pretty hair-raising. "No worries. You know I've always got your back."

"No, Darla, you've always got everyone's back. I owe you."

Born To Lose

Jacqueline

This is it. This is my last attempt at a normal date. This one will start differently than the others and it will end differently as well, else I will join a convent.

Bobby is already unlike any other guy I've met. He owns an art gallery in Santa Monica. I'm not much of an art aficionado (At best, I can tell a Picasso from a Rembrandt—maybe.), but we have other things in common, like star gazing and cheesy carnival rides. Every great romance has to start somewhere, right?

The bell over the door tinkles as I walk into the gallery. The place is dark with the exception of how each side is lined with small spotlights that point up to illuminate rows of statues. The golden glows light my path, yet make the place spooky. The clicks of my heels bounce off the walls and aid in making me feel ill at ease. "Bobby?" I call out in search of my date. The place stays silent. He said to meet him here at seven, and it is now five minutes after.

I call out again and get no answer.

The bell on the door tinkles, and I turn to face the man whose profile I looked at just this morning—the man with whom I set a date for this evening—the man who is holding hands with another woman. His eyes widen.

Great, just what I need, more scum. At least this one was caught in the act—sort of. He looks to the woman and motions to a room off to the side. She looks like she is going in to give him a kiss on the cheek but instead takes a playful nip at his ear. "Don't keep me waiting," she says with a wink.

What do I do now? Storm out? Stop her and tell her I am his date? Maybe she knows and it's all a game to get a threesome. Not knowing what else to do, I take two steps forward, extend my hand, and introduce myself. "Hi, I'm Jacqueline, the one you made a date with for tonight."

Bobby shakes my hand, and then scrapes his hand through his hair, scratching as he goes. His eyes go to the alcove where the door to the other room lies. "I uh …"

"I was thinking we would go to that cute, little coffee shop next door. Would that be all right?"

The woman steps into the alcove where there is just enough light to see she is unbuttoning her blouse. She drops it on the floor and reaches behind her to undo her bra before turning back to where she came from.

Finally, Bobby's eyes go to mine. "You have to leave."

Yeah, no kidding. I've no intention of staying, but if I simply leave, he gets away with treating me like scum. I decide to play dumb, because I am really curious as to what he will say. "But we had plans."

"Yeah, but uh …"

"I'm waiting," comes from the other room.

"Sorry, you need to go." Bobby guides me toward the front door. I dig my heels in and stop.

"I'm sorry. Did I have the date wrong? We did say today, didn't we?"

"I don't know what you are talking about. You must have me mistaken for someone else."

I look around. "Hmm … I could have sworn the sign on the door said Hunter's Gallery. You are Bobby Hunter, aren't you?"

The woman reemerges with her bra back on. She swipes up her blouse and starts to leave. Bobby gives me a shove toward the door. "I'm sorry, we are closed. Kindly come back tomorrow, and I will have a price on that piece for you." He then takes the woman's arm and guides her toward the back while unbuttoning his shirt. He tosses it to the ground and goes for his buckle while following the woman in haste.

What the hell? No, whatever is going on with my bad luck in dating, I am definitely not the problem!

I head out with the intention of not looking back. How many times will bad luck prevail? Maybe I should have stood up to that guy and ratted him out. Then again, I don't think that woman cared much. What matters is that I wussed out.

A soft voice comes up from near my feet. "Spare some change?" Sitting with his back to a trashcan is a man who looks like he has not eaten in days. How he cowers with his head down like he has lost all dignity makes my heart hurt all the more for him. He's hard to look at, and my eyes divert without my permission.

What kind of person am I? This guy does not seem to want a fix; he wants a meal and probably a shower. I'm on my way home to sulk in luxury with my best friend while he sits on the hot pavement, baking in the sun and probably feeling alone and hungry.

Not if I have anything to say about it.

I plop down next to him—straight onto the filthy, spat-on, and gum-discarded-on sidewalk. He turns to me—a dolled-up woman whom he probably expected not to give him so much as a glare—and looks bewildered.

"I just lost some dignity," I tell him. "Want to help me get it back?"

He does not seem fazed. "Lady, I know all about having a lack of dignity. That's the one thing no one should ever lose. What do you need?"

"Your voice for about ten seconds."

"You got it."

Wow. He is not even asking if I am going to pay him? I tell him what happened and give him my instructions. He smiles and starts to get up. I tell him to hold up a second.

From the ATM down the block, I withdraw two hundred dollars. He would probably be thrilled with ten, but this money will do him far more good that it would me.

I give him the cash, in advance. His eyes turn into wells that nearly burst. Tears come into my eyes too, and I realize that my dignity has already returned. I could stop now and be good.

Yeah, maybe I have taken this far enough.

I start to head off, and he follows right along side me. "I see that look in your eyes," he says. "Don't back down. I'm doing this with or without you. You should at least stick around to enjoy it."

Okay, I am in it this far, and he is willing, so I look up and smile.

When we get to the gallery door I nod that this is the place. He takes two steps back, puts on his game face, and runs so that he can burst through the door with force. From inside the gallery moans of pleasure fill the air, that is, until the guy yells, "Fire! The building is on fire! Fire!"

I hold the door open as he bursts out and tears down the street. Bobby and his date run out, completely naked, and well, damp. From the looks of things, (actually, from the look of his thing) he had not quite finished yet.

Bobby stares at me wide-eyed. He then clues in and starts huffing.

"Are you ready for our date now?" I ask.

As I laugh my way down the street I realize that I was right about one thing: this date definitely ended differently than the others.

Work-A-Day World

Rosalyn

My workday has been filled with so many computer problems, exploding coffee machines, and co-worker induced lameness that this call from Jacqueline is just the icing on the cake. "Maybe the drama in my personal life is getting me to look at all areas of my life too closely," she says. "My job is really not that bad, it's just that I'm unfulfilled and not seeing any room for advancement. My chances would be better if I were in the same position elsewhere."

The tone in Jacqueline's voice translates stronger than her words. I totally get it. We are both wasting away in our current jobs. The fact that I am again rebooting my computer that keeps locking up reinforces that. "It's the same here. I love the people I work with, but this isn't the life I want."

"Then let's go on a quest and start our own business. With your degree in business and mine in marketing we are already part of the way there. Let's start saving money with the plan that the moment we find the right avenue, we hop on it! Are you with me?"

Jacqueline and I always pick one up when the other is down, but if she is just trying to console me during a tough day at work, this pep talk is a little heavy handed. "Jacqueline, this isn't just some crazy idea to get my mind off of everything, is it?" Darla dashes in while waiving a piece of paper and motioning me to cover my mouthpiece.

"No, Rox. I am dead serious," Jacqueline continues as Darla smacks the paper on my desk. "We're always talking about taking chances. Frankly, this isn't just to boost you, it's to boost me as well. We've spent decades growing up together. Let's not stop now."

Darla whispers, "Guess who is here completing his employee orientation package." She points to the résumé for the hot guy that came in here a few days ago—the one she held on to just in case he was *needed*. "Think Jacqueline would like him?"

I adamantly nod. With all the stability on that résumé and his desire to move forward, yeah, there's a damn good chance she would. Darla is brilliant!

Something in my brain clicks. No, Darla's not brilliant, she's ingenious! She and Jacqueline may have just planted a seed for our futures.

My computer finally does something definitive in the form of presenting me with the blue screen of death. Omens surround me, and I'd be a fool not to get my head out of my butt and act. I look to Darla while speaking to both her and Jacqueline. "Okay, I'm in. Start dreaming. Jacqueline, I'll talk to you later. Some very important paperwork just crossed my desk." I can't hang up fast enough. "Darla, you talked to this guy when he came in before, right?"

"Yep."

"What exactly did you two chat about?"

Darla takes the extra chair I keep across the room and pulls up a seat next to me. "Well, it started pretty simply about the type of work he had done in the past. Once we started talking about changes, he just sort of opened up about all of the ones he had been through with losing his wife a few years ago. He then had to learn that it was okay to wait to find it within himself to start over. Now he's ready to do that in all aspects of his life."

Right there is the golden ticket: talking. It's something we as a society don't do enough of, and it's the only way to get to know someone. "So basically you feel good about introducing this guy to one of your best friends because you had a real conversation with him?"

Darla shrugs. "Yeah, that and the fact that I just checked his work references. Everything he told me blended with what his past employer said. Davion is a good guy who lost everything that meant anything to him, and now he is ready to find a new version of it. Those are his words, not mine. Why? Are you afraid he's not good enough for Jacqueline?"

This is perfect. Like *really* perfect! "Darla, if you think he is a great catch for her, so do I. In fact, how would you feel about going into business doing exactly what you just did?"

"Huh?"

"The reason dating services are so cheesy is because anyone can fake any background they want and play that game until they slip and let their true colors show. When people apply for jobs, the process is not as lenient. Granted, people can still lie and get away with it, but it is not nearly as easy. Jacqueline doesn't know it yet, but she and I are about to form a dating agency. Want to join us?"

Darla cocks an eyebrow. "Agency?"

"Yes. Dating services provide a way for people to meet. Employment agencies make employee/employer matches based on references and interviews. If you combine the two—"

Darla smacks her hand on my desk. "Then you get something as brilliant as what I just did."

"I could not have said it better myself!"

Darla leans in and whispers. "You really think we can do it and get the hell out of here?"

"Not only do I know we can, but I am certain that the time is now. You in?"

Darla high-fives me. "In!"

Even Better Than The Real Thing

Jacqueline

When Rosalyn and I reach Mulligan's for our normal, Friday night out, Darla is already here and has ordered for all of us. She looks … awkward—not out of place, not sick, and not like anything is wrong, just … awkward.

"Are you okay?" I ask her.

"Great. Why?" She nearly races to grab a sip of her cocktail. Her eyes dart over to the bar, then back on to the drink.

"Why are you looking around the bar? Are you expecting someone?"

"Nope, just checking out the scenery."

Something is definitely up. As much as misery loves company, I really hope that I won't soon have a partner in the lonely hearts club. "Why? I thought you were happy. You're not giving up on Chris already, are you?"

"Nah, everything is great." Her smile reaches into my heart and tugs at it.

I give Darla's arm a squeeze. "I'm really happy for you." I want my friends to be happy, even if it means having lonely nights of being single while they are out on dates.

Laughter fills the room from behind me. Darla peers toward it. I start to turn my head, but I get distracted when she smacks on the table. "Did you hear about the latest pranks that Oliver and I played on each other?"

"Lord, what now?" Rosalyn asks. "You didn't follow through on your threat to exchange sweetener packets with salt in them for the ones he uses in his coffee, did you?"

"God, what is it with you two?" I ask. I take another sip of my drink. Should I order another, or should I suggest we bail? I need something different. Maybe we should all go home, get our bags, and head off to Mexico.

Darla pulls her purse off of the back of her chair and searches out a tube of lipstick. She then rummages for a mirror. "Well, I had to come up with something clever after he gave me—"

Darla slams her hand onto the table and shoves something toward me. My heart starts racing at the sight of what looks like a giant, plastic spider. Spiders freak me out, big time! I know it is not real, yet I can't help but jerk back and jump off of my seat so it won't land in my lap. Someone is behind me, and I try to right myself from toppling down. My efforts are futile and I land in a pair of arms.

I fight the urge to rip Darla a new one so I can apologize to whomever I just bumped into. I turn and look up into—

Oh, dear God. Those eyes.

Before me are the most gorgeous, brown eyes I've ever seen, not just because they are heavenly, but something about them says that they are attached to a beautiful soul. They are more breath stealing than the fake spider that scared the crap out of me.

"Hi," he says with those eyes locked into mine.

My "hi" sounds like I am breathless. Emotionally, I am.

The eyes pull back, and I find they belong to a man who is tall and dark featured. Oh, Lord. Those cheek bones. They are so chiseled that I have to fight the urge to run my hand over them.

My God. This man has me absolutely floored. The energy coming off of him is so sweet and endearing. I don't want him to release me from his arms, not because they are strong, but because his embrace feels safe.

A familiar voice approaches. "Hey, guys. What's all the ruckus about?" Oliver slaps the guy who caught me on the back.

Oliver? Oliver from Rosalyn and Darla's work? He knows

this guy?

Oh no! She did not! Son of a bitch, Darla totally set me up. "You all work together?" I ask.

"Yeah," Darla says. "I asked a few people to join us. I figured we all needed a little party." She picks up her glass and sips like nothing's out of the ordinary. She then shoots me a wink. I kind of want to kill her, but I have to hand it to her. Of all the ways to set me up, this was brilliant.

Darla and Rosalyn introduce me to a few of the crew from their work that I have not already met at previous gatherings. "I can see you've met Davion," Darla adds at the end. There's that sly look again. She heads to the table next to us and butts it against ours. She's not leaving any room for errors. We are all sitting together, whether we like it or not.

Davion looks to the empty chair that Darla sets next to me and asks if I mind if he sits there. I motion towards it and say to be my guest. I then turn to Rosalyn who is trying to hide her grin behind her drink. Damn, is she in on this too? As if reading my mind, she leans in and whispers in my ear, "This was all Darla's doing. She's right on this one. If you don't ignore the rest of us tonight and focus completely on this guy, you're absolutely crazy." She leans back, takes a sip of her cocktail, and smiles.

Rosalyn and Darla start a high-five and hug fest, and then start giggling. Oliver plops down in the seat next to Rosalyn. "What are we talking about?" he asks.

Darla manages to keep a straight face when she lies and says, "The spray glue I put on that chair before you walked in." Oliver jumps up to check his pants. And so the harassment begins.

I turn to Davion who looks at me and smiles. "So, Jacqueline, tell me something wonderful about the world."

I like this guy already.

The Way You Look Tonight

Jacqueline

I pull back the clasp on a strand of pearls, then wrap it around my neck. The hook is just about to slip into the hole when—

Snap!

Darn it! "Again? Really?"

Rosalyn sticks her head into my room. "You okay," she asks.

"Yes, just inept." I hold up the strand and plead for help. She secures it around my neck without the need of more appendages. I close my eyes, gather a breath, and give it a long exhale. "Thank you."

Rosalyn giggles, plops onto my bed, and kicks her legs out. "Ooh! Cute outfit. You look all snazzy!" I spin to face the mirror. Did I over-do it? I want to look nice, but I don't want to look like a tramp. My arms may be mostly bare, but my cleavage is covered. Well, mostly covered. And you can see my knees but— "Relax," she tells me. "Snazzy is not code for whore. You look fantastic. Why the stress?"

Busted. I take a seat next to her. "Because I am lame. This is technically a first date, and while the initial meeting the other night went well, as have the following phone conversations, that does not change the fact that this is a first date. I don't know if you have noticed, but first dates and I don't exactly mesh."

The doorbell rings, and I just about jump. Rosalyn laughs. "Relax! Take a minute to gather yourself while I get the door." She starts to head out. "Davion is a nice guy, not some freak." Suddenly she stops and spins around. "Or so we think. You know, come to think of it, I did see him eating some of the candy we make at work. Anyone who does that must be psychotic. I'll tell him you came down with the plague and spare you from breaking your bad luck streak."

"Not funny, Rox. Please tell him I'll be down in a minute."

Again, she starts to head out while I look in the full-length mirror. Suddenly Rosalyn stops again. "Hey, hold on," she says while looking at my rear end.

I spin my back toward the mirror. Do I have something on my—

Rosalyn smacks my butt. "Nice tush. Now get your head out of it and go have a good time."

She's right. Giving myself the once-over sixteen times was fifteen times too many and thirteen times more than is sane. "Stay here," I tell her. "With the mood you are in, if you answer the door, you are sure to say something to embarrass me." I grab my purse and give Rosalyn a kiss on the cheek before heading down the stairs and yelling, "Good night, Mom."

❈

Davion stares at his menu. From the moment he picked me up, his eyes have been anywhere but on me. In a way it is refreshing. However, it is also increasing my jitters. I've also been so nervous that I have not been able to look at him either.

I need to suck it up. I'll ask a question while mustering the courage, and then I will look straight at him while listening to the answer. "The Chicken Piccata looks good," I muse. "I'm kind of torn between it and the Lamb Medallions. Have you decided yet?" I look up.

He sighs. "No, too many choices." Still he remains tucked away.

"I might have a dart in my purse. Wanna borrow it?"

He chuckles and then … nothing.

What happened to the man whose first thing he said to me was a request to tell him something wonderful about the world? Things had gone so well that night. They have also gone well every time since when we have talked over the phone. The only thing I can do is face that when it comes to dates, I'm cursed.

Was it crazy to break my rule of taking my own car? It's not like we are total strangers. The other night at Mulligan's we slipped into a private booth and spent hours talking about everything from the weather to philosophies on life. That has to count for something, and therefore this is not really a first date.

It's not really a second date either. I guess this is kind of date one point five.

Gah! This is not helping matters any!

Davion speaks, yet his menu remains in place. "Why did you have to go and say lamb? I was doing fine until then. Now I can't decide between that and the Penne in Vodka Sauce." Finally he puts down the menu, only to stare at the wall. "Truthfully, I really want the lamb, but if I order it now, it'll look like I am following your lead. If you get something else and think my lamb looks better, I'll feel obligated to switch. If you get the lamb and it looks better than what I get, I'll kick myself."

I turn to look at the wall, right where he is staring. It's a solid, peach-colored wall. I know I did not dress over the top, but is the wall really more interesting?

When I turn back around, Davion's eyes are on me. We smile and hold the eye contact. Ah, so much better.

"This is ridiculous," he says. "You seem like a normal, sane woman. Your friends are normal." He rethinks that, as he well should. "Well, somewhat normal. So there is no reason why I can't just relax, right?"

I exhale in relief. "Yes."

"Great. Then it should also be okay for me to say something I have wanted since the moment I picked you up but have shamefully neglected to do. The thing is, the last time

I said something like this, I nearly lost my man parts."

My insides clench. Dare I want to know what almost made a woman rip his balls off? He opens his lips, and I hope the restroom has a window for me to slip out of.

"Jacqueline," he says softly, "you look lovely."

I swallow back how touched I am and take a moment to enjoy the compliment. But the lead in and the comment don't make sense together. "That got you in trouble with someone?"

"Yes, and since now it seems that you are not speed balling into anger, I'd like to tell you the rest of what I am thinking." That same, soul-gripping warmth that I saw in him the night we met returns. "Truthfully, I have met some very beautiful women, but there is something about you that is stunning beyond words. You are the epitome of elegance."

My face warms, and I have to divert my eyes due to self-consciousness. I have no idea how to respond, or even if I should. I am so touched that it is all I can do to say, "Thank you." I fuss with my napkin, and then take a sip of water. I peer up at him and smile, but then I have to ask, "How could telling someone she looks nice get you in trouble?"

Davion's eyes roll to heaven. "You would not believe the trouble I get into!"

Oh no.

His gaze then darts to mine, and his hands fly out in a halting motion. "That sounded really bad. It's just that, I've had terrible luck with first dates. It's only been a short time since I've gotten back into the dating game, but let me tell you, every date so far has been a doozy! The last woman I told she looked nice flipped out about how I was only saying that because she was wearing a dress. She went on and on about how if she were not showing some leg, no man would say a word about the result of the three hours she spent getting ready for a date. Three hours! Then I made the mistake of asking if she was really telling the truth about how long it took. Lord, you would have thought I had accused her of murder!"

Now it all makes so much sense. "Is this why you have

been so easy to talk to all along, yet tonight you have a hard time looking at me?"

"I know it sounds ridiculous, but in a word, yes."

I toss my hands to God. "Thank you!" When I look back to Davion, he is laughing.

"Oh no, not you too."

"Where should I start? How about the time a guy swore up and down, while basically drooling, that I had to be a biter because I wore black? I then got badgered over what blood types taste best. Or how about the time when I didn't wear black? I had to slip out of a restaurant and catch a bus without my freak-show date noticing."

"Oh, man!" he says. "Start with the biter and then I'll follow it with the time I got pinned to a wall and had black lipstick smeared on me, and no, not via her lips."

I am so relieved to have found a kindred spirit. With that in mind, I have to take one, very important, precaution. "Sure, but before that, let's agree on one thing. This is not a first date, because the second either of us agrees that it is, we are doomed."

"It's a deal."

Davion and I spend hours sharing stories, so much so that we miss our film and wind up closing down the restaurant. They say everything happens for a reason. Finally, I can buy into that. All those bad dates weren't in vain after all.

Instant Karma

Three Months Later

Jacqueline

Is there such a thing as luck? What about karma? Were the months of dating hell I went through payback for some wrong I did years before? Did I then do something to make good karma step in and send my bad luck in the other direction? Was it when I decided that helping a homeless man was more important than payback to a creep who ditched me? Any way I look at the events that got me here, just twenty minutes ago, Rosalyn and I signed the final paperwork, thus forming our new business, Cupid's Stardust—an agency for those who want more out of life and are not afraid to seek it.

I pull into the driveway at Mulligan's, ready to celebrate with my friends. Davion stands out front with a bouquet of pink roses—bright, beautiful, *unpainted*, pink roses. I smile in memory of the day I was given a black one. I kind of wish I still had it. It would have been the perfect symbol of success to hang on the wall of my future office.

Davion greets me with a congratulatory kiss that sends my heart aflutter. When I pull back and see those eyes that send me over the moon, I just about melt into the concrete.

With his hand in mine, we head inside. While we have only known each other for three months, they have been a whirlwind of happiness. I won't go so far as to say he is the one I will spend forever with, yet my inner voice screams that he is.

Inside the darkened bar I breathe in the glorious, stale air.

I used to think this place was a pit, but now I see it for what it is: a place where magic happens.

Does Mulligan's really possess magic? Read more about Rosalyn, Niles, Jacqueline, and Darla in *Scary Modsters … and Creepy Freaks*, and its prequel, *It's A Marshmallow World*. Next, follow Darla into the companion novel, *Voices Carry*. A mystery waits.

Playlist

"King Midas In Reverse" - The Hollies
"Love Stinks" - J. Giles Band
"Not Fade Away" - The Rolling Stones
"Born Under A Bad Sign" - The Cream
"Girl All the Bad Boys Want" - Bowling For Soup
"Oliver's Army" - Elvis Costello and the Attractions
"Born To Lose" - Johnny Thunders
"Work-A-Day World" - The Beat
"Even Better Than The Real Thing" - U2
"The Way You Look Tonight" - Frank Sinatra
"Instant Karma! (We All Shine On)" - Lennon/Ono (with the Plastic Ono Band)

MORE BY DIANE RINELLA

THE ROCK AND ROLL FANTASY COLLECTION

Scary Modsters…and Creepy Freaks
It's A Marshmallow World
Voices Carry
Moonlight Serenade

SOMETHING TO DREAM ON

THE FORBIDDEN FLOWER SERIES

Love's Forbidden Flower
Time's Forbidden Flower

About The Author

Enjoying San Francisco as a backdrop, the ghosts in USA Today Bestselling Author Diane Rinella's 150-year old Victorian home augment the chorus in her head. With insomnia as their catalyst, these voices have become multifarious characters that haunt her well into the sun's crowning hours, refusing to let go until they have manipulated her into succumbing to their whims. Her experiences as an actress, business owner, artisan cake designer, software project manager, Internet radio disc jockey, vintage rock n' roll journalist/fan girl, and lover of dark and quirky personalities influence her idiosyncratic writing.

You can visit her website at www.dianerinellaauthor.com and on Facebook at https://www.facebook.com/DianeRinellaAuthor/